Farmer Bloom &
The Magic Worms

It doesn't stop here,
follow the magical journey at
wormsaremagic.com

Copyright © Scott Bloom & Roz Murphy, 2021.

All rights reserved. No part of this book may be reproduced or used in any manner without the prior written permission of the copyright owner, except for the use of brief quotations in a book review.

Edition 01; March 20, 2021.

Written for Samari and Jacob.
Drawn with love for Kati.

One day, Diana visited Farmer Bloom. He was making a fuss about some tomatoes.

Diana was amazed and asked "How do you grow such beautiful tomatoes?"

Farmer Bloom said "Can I tell you a secret? It's the magic worms."

Confused and curious, Diana said "Magic worms? ... tell me more about that."

It started on a very hot day last summer...

...There was a knock at the door. When Farmer Bloom answered, he saw three worms. They didn't look so great.

The worms cried "It's so hot outside! We're dry and need water to breathe. If you give us shelter, water and food for the summer, we will help you grow the best garden ever! Children's books will be written about you! Please, we just need some dirt and water in a small cup and we'll show you how to make a worm bin for us."

Farmer Bloom found an old, empty pot. He put in dirt, a little water, and a bit of fruit.

Able to finally breathe through their skin. The worms nibbled on scraps from the garden. They began to cool off from being in the hot sun.

The worms were happy and safe.

The next day, the worms became very, very serious!

"The most important thing to know is that we need water mixed into the dirt. It's how we breathe through our skin. If we're too dry, we can't breathe!"

"Get a plastic bin and poke holes in it. Fill the bin with dirt from your garden. Find some paper, tear it into small pieces. Then add water and use your hands to mix everything together.

Our favorite foods are apple cores, tomato pieces and pumpkins.

Once we've climbed into the bin, make sure you keep it covered with wet paper and a lid to keep the flies out!"

Then the worms crawled into the bin and wiggled their way into the dirt. Farmer Bloom checked on his worm friends every couple of days. He added more water and food to keep his worms happy and healthy. More worms began to appear. He noticed the dirt beginning to change. It was getting darker, almost like magic.

As the weeks passed, Farmer Bloom kept an eye on the worms to make sure their home had plenty of food and water.

For the worms, this was paradise. They grew in numbers, and always celebrated the seasons.

The worms were leaving behind a dark, magical soil. The worms told Farmer Bloom to add the magical soil to his own garden. So he added it to all the plants in his greenhouse, including the tomatoes.

As time moved on, summer became fall, and fall turned into winter. When winter started to warm up, and the days began to get longer, the worms, as if by magic, knew it was time...

Every day Farmer Bloom was surprised by the growing magic.

Farmer Bloom couldn't believe how much better his garden looked, thanks to his magical worms.

And best of all, his tomatoes were the biggest and most colorful he had ever seen.

"It was this time last year that you gave us the gift of food, water, and a home. The plants are our way of saying **thank you**."

"So you see, the worms are magic. Would you like to go meet them?" asked Farmer Bloom. The worm looked up from his food scrap and said, "We are excited to help you with your garden next spring!"

"Oh!" said Diana "I guess they can talk."

The End

...

Or is it?
Follow the magical journey at
wormsaremagic.com
@farmer_bloom

Thank you to our friends and family for your support, insights, and patience to help make this book become a reality: Jeshka Y., Megan M., Erin W., Diana O., and Kati M.

xoxo

Scott & Roz

Made in the USA
Coppell, TX
30 August 2021